Alicia's Treasure

Diane Gonzales Bertrand

PIÑATA
BOOKS

PIÑATA BOOKS
HOUSTON, TEXAS
1996

This volume is made possible through grants from the National Endowment for the Arts (a federal agency) and the Andrew W. Mellon Foundation.

Piñata Books are full of surprises!

Piñata Books
An Imptint of Arte Público Press
University of Houston
452 Cullen Performance Hall
Houston, Texas 77204-2004

Cover design by Gladys Ramirez

Cover art piece and illustrations by Daniel Lechón

Bertrand, Diane Gonzales.
   Alicia's treasure / by Diane Gonzales Bertrand.
     p.   cm.
   Summary: When ten-year-old Alicia accompanies her brother and his girl friend to the beach, she experiences many things for the first time and gains new insights into herself.
   ISBN 1-55885-086-4 (paper : alk. paper)
   [1. Brothers and sisters—Fiction. 2. Beaches—Fiction. 3. Mexican Americans—Fiction.] I. Title.
PZ7.B46357A1   1995
[Fic]—dc20   95-37669
                                        CIP
                                        AC

   2 3 4 5 6 7 8 9 0   13 12 11 10 9 8 7 6

To Sister Ann Semel, S.S.N.D.
and
For Nicky and Suzanne

Contents

Alicia's Treasure

Chapter One
From the Back Seat

I suppose this could be just another girl goes to the beach story. Except for one thing. I'm Alicia Inez Ramos. My story will be different.

I've had three hours stuck in the back seat of my brother Sergio's car to plan every moment of the weekend. I feel like I've waited all my life for this trip. I know I'm not the only ten-year-old who hasn't seen the beach. But I'm the one in this story. The one in the back seat who first sees the words, Aransas Pass Bridge.

As Sergio's car comes down the other side of the high bridge, I can hardly keep my seat belt on.

I push my nose against the window to take my first look at the ocean. It looks blue with a grayish top, wrinkled by little waves. Where there's no water, I see sandy ground. The sand seems almost white under the sunshine.

Then, it all disappears into a fog.

I have to wipe my breath off the window before I can look at everything again. And I know it's not enough, not for me.

I start cranking down the back seat window.

Hot air smashes into my face. My long hair flies back. I close my eyes and take a good long smell.

"Hey! Alicia! Put the window up!" Sergio yells.

"I want to smell the ocean," I answer as I crank the window all the way down. I take a long, noisy sniff. I can't tell much. It's hard to catch any smells because the wind comes through the window too fast.

"Alicia, I got the air-conditioner on! Put the window up! Now!" Sergio yells louder.

I give him a dirty look. I know he was born just to spoil my fun.

"Oh, Sergio. Leave Alicia alone," Carmen says. She's sitting next to him in the front seat. Her red painted fingernails wiggle through the back of Sergio's black hair. "Alicia's never been to the beach before. Let her smell the ocean if she wants."

Sergio mutters something. Carmen giggles. Sometimes, I wonder how my brother got so lucky to have a girlfriend like her.

Actually, Carmen is the reason I'm sitting in the back seat today.

She and Sergio have been dating since Christmas. I think she's great. Nothing like any of Sergio's other girlfriends. She talks to me like I'm a person, not a pest. I almost feel like she's the sister I never got.

During the time Carmen has spent around our house, she's talked some about her family. One day she mentioned her parents' summer trips to Port Aransas and all the fun they have on the beach. My parents' idea of vacation is a trip to Mexico to see my relatives. We've got a lot of relatives, so we take a lot of trips, but always and only to Mexico. What would it be like to take a car trip and see something new?

Since I kept asking questions about the beach, I guess Carmen felt sorry for me. When she invited Sergio to come with her family this summer, she asked me if I wanted to come too.

I can still remember Sergio's face. He has a brown face, but that night it turned a grayish color, then kind of purple, then red.

I know he didn't want me to tag along, but he couldn't say much and not sound like a total jerk in front of Carmen. She always talks real nice about her brothers and sister.

Not me and Sergio. He's bossy and selfish. And he thinks I'm stupid. So why would I want to spend two days with him at the beach? Hey! I would have agreed to spend the weekend with Godzilla just for a chance to see the beach for myself.

I really think Sergio expected Mom and Dad to say, "No." Dad especially. He still treats me like a baby. But I came up with a plan to get around Mom and Dad. I got Carmen to talk to my folks. They really like her. Then, she got her mother to call my mother. When I heard Mom speaking in Spanish with Mrs. Sandoval like two *comadres*, I knew then, I had it made. Port Aransas, here I come!

Once they agreed to let me go, Sergio heard nothing but, "Take care of your sister." He rolled his eyes every time Mom started talking. I know he wishes I wasn't going along. Well, I don't exactly want him around either.

When Carmen mentioned taking the road that would let us ride the ferry boat, I wanted to ask Mom and Dad to make Sergio promise he wouldn't toss me in the Gulf, but I kept quiet. I didn't want to give him any ideas.

And with all the excitement of getting permission to go with Carmen's family, I was still worried about Sergio. Without Mom or Dad around, would he get too bossy? Would I still be able to have fun?

For most of this three-hour drive, Sergio has pretended that I'm not around. Not until I rolled down the window and let a little air into his car. Okay. I guess I can smell the ocean later. I roll up the window. At least I can look at it. I could be just sitting at home.

"Look, Alicia. See those posts?"

I follow a red fingernail and look out the other window. I see an uneven row of poles sticking out of the water.

"My grandfather told me the poles supported a one way bridge, but the hurricanes knocked them down," Carmen tells me.

So? Looks like a bunch of telephone poles with no wires to me. I glance from side to side as Sergio drives down the two-lane highway. I keep waiting for something wonderful. All I see is the same bluish water with weak waves. And the land around us is mostly sand with patches of skinny brown weeds. It's nothing like I've seen on TV.

Where are the surfers riding big waves? Where are the happy children who build sand castles on the beach? Where are the old men with skinny white legs looking for shells? I don't see any big fishing boats lowering rope nets for shrimp and lobsters. I don't see sharks or whales. I see more phone poles, a couple of rusty house trailers and a wooden shack that sells bait. Some beach.

Then, I see this sign. PORT ARANSAS 15 MILES.

So we aren't really at the place where Carmen says her parents spend their vacation. We're still trying to get there. It's still fifteen miles away.

Suddenly, Sergio starts singing with the music on the radio. He sounds like one of Tío Chale's squawking chickens, only no one's going to cut off Sergio's head and roast him for supper.

I lean back into the seat and tell myself this trip will be the best one in my life.

Even if I have to share it with Sergio.

Chapter Two
The Ferry Boat

The car slows suddenly, then jerks to a stop. I bounce against the back seat.

"What's going on?" I unbuckle my seat belt so I can lean up to the front.

All I see is a big red propeller. It blocks the entire windshield of Sergio's car. Then, I see the propeller is hooked to a white boat being pulled by a green truck.

"Gosh, we left so early." Carmen speaks in a soft voice. "I thought we could avoid the traffic waiting for the ferry."

Sergio makes a sound like a pig. "I told you we should have gone through Corpus Christi. But, no! You said Alicia had to ride the ferry."

"It's part of the fun, Sergio."

"Some fun." Sergio reaches out and turns off the air-conditioner. He rolls down his window. "We'll spend half the day in line."

Carmen's red nails start wiggling through Sergio's hair again. "I'm sure all the ferries are running today. It won't be long. Alicia, why don't you try and smell the ocean now?"

I roll down the window and take a deep breath. I start coughing. The only thing I can smell is the stuff coming out of the truck pulling the boat in front of us. I wrinkle my nose. Maybe later. I slide down in my seat and wait.

We seem to move along, then jerk to a stop for hours and hours. I keep looking at my watch. It's really been just fifteen minutes. As we move down the road, I see a field with huge silver tanks built upon it. Out the other window, I see these big iron cones lying on their sides. From where I sit, it looks like the workman are the size of ants.

"What do they use those towers for?" I ask.

"They are platforms to drill oil, " Sergio says. "They build them on shore, then pull them out into the ocean."

I remember Mrs. Martinez, our science teacher, talking about oil spills in the ocean, and the way the oil kills the fish and messes up the beach. I'm about to say something to

Sergio about it, so he'll know I'm not as stupid as he thinks, when the car moves around the curve.

I can finally see the ferry boats carrying the cars across the water. Nothing else matters now.

The ferries are flat boats with short walls on each side to keep the cars in, and metal gates across the front and back. I see a white tower in the middle and two rows of cars on each side. Men in gray uniforms wave cars onto the boat. One man signals at Sergio to drive forward. I'm so excited that my stomach feels like it's doing cartwheels.

Sergio's car is the first one in the last row. He stops his car at the front railing, and then I hear Carmen say, "Come on, Alicia!"

She moves away from Sergio and opens the car door.

I climb over the folded-down front seat and step onto the boat.

My legs are stiff from sitting so long in the car. The floor moves under my feet. The wind slaps my long hair into my face. I grab it in one hand and wobble along the car at the same time. I finally get to where Sergio and Carmen are standing.

I hear cries of birds. Squinting into the sunshine, I see birds flying around the boat. Some are grey, but most are white with brown wings and skinny black beaks. One comes diving down in our direction, and I duck my head.

I hear Sergio and Carmen laughing at me.

"Sea gulls won't hurt you," Carmen says. "They just want to eat."

She tosses a couple of chips at the birds. First one bird, then another, catches a chip in its beak. They continue to fly around the spot, making screechy sounds, but Carmen shrugs and laughs.

"Sorry, birdies. Sergio ate most of them."

I start looking around the channel at the ships parked beside the big docks made of telephone pole posts. I see a red tugboat and a flat iron boat with a fat smoke stack. Then, I see other ferry boats passing one another.

Feeling more comfortable walking on a swaying floor, I go to the edge of the ferry. I hold onto the dark metal gate which will keep our car from falling in. Looking into the water, I still can't decide its color. I bend

over for a closer look, feeling the mist of salty water on my face.

Suddenly the boat jerks. The floor beneath my feet moves too quickly for me to get my balance. "Sergio!"

I screech louder than a sea gull. Somebody grabs me by the shorts. I get jerked backwards and bump into the front of the car.

"You crazy kid." Sergio's eyes are like shiny black rocks. "Do you want to fall in or what?"

"I wanted to look at the water." Even as I say it, I feel pretty stupid. I almost fell in when the boat moved. I can swim, sure. But in a deep ocean? I just turn away and walk to the side of the ferry boat, trying not to show how embarrassed I feel. I reach out and grab tightly to the railing, trying to make my heart stop thumping so hard.

I raise my head up, feeling a salty taste in my mouth. I wonder where it comes from. Then I realize that taste comes from breathing the air. I sniff a salty smell with a definite fishy odor, but it's not too bad. The breeze tingles on my cheeks. All that wet air cools the sun shining on my shoulders.

Inside my head, my mother's voice sounds loud and clear, *Don't forget to put on a lot of sunscreen lotion.* I wonder what Mom's doing at home right now.

The ferry boat's motor seems to get louder. Carmen's calling to me to get back into the car. The boat's about to glide into another dock made of black poles tied together. We all climb back into the car. I watch the front gate unfold into a ramp which lays upon the dock. Sergio's car bounces the ramp onto the dock as we drive over. We're back on land again.

A blue water tank painted with a giant swordfish tells us: WELCOME TO PORT ARANSAS, TEXAS.

Chapter Three
On Vacation

Port Aransas. I'm not sure where to look first. Wooden buildings on one side sell bait, hamburgers, and souvenirs. Near the water, I see these two-story condominiums built up on stilts and fancy boats parked underneath them. I pretend I'm living in one of those places riding my boat whenever I want. I'm waving at fishermen, or I go out and catch a fish as big as I am. And Sergio is nowhere around me.

I count the two-story houses we pass, and hope we'll stop at one of these, but we don't. We keep driving. Suddenly, the air stinks like dead fish. As we turn at the traffic signal, we pass a place where fishing boats are lined up. I start to wonder again. Where is the beach?

I look around as we drive down a main street, and see places to eat and souvenir shops with wild pink fish nets and tall plaster shells. A row of T-shirts covers the side of one store, and there's a full set of armor out-side another shop shaped like a pirate ship.

I realize I should be taking pictures of all this. I remember the camera's in my suit-case in the trunk. Sergio said I wouldn't need it until we got to the beach, but he was wrong. There are so many things I want to remember.

Carmen starts telling Sergio when and where to turn. We pass three motels with swimming pools as he turns off.

I see all kind of houses. Some are painted alike and have a sign like BEACH COMBER COURTS. I see individual houses up on stilts with garages or carports to park boats and cars, and in between are unpainted small shacks which look like the bait shops I saw before we crossed the ferry. I see one house made of the same black wood as the docks. And there are more of those long, brown weeds instead of grass.

I look around, still waiting to see the beach. All I see are houses.

Finally, Carmen says, "We're here."

I look out the window at a small, square house that looks no different from any other in my neighborhood. This one's painted mustard yellow. The white wooden porch leans to one side.

When Carmen said her parents always rented a place at the beach, I was thinking of a carpeted apartment with a balcony where I could look out at the ocean and could walk out the front door and feel the sand between my toes. Whenever I wanted I could walk to the beach and find treasures in the sand. I could swim in the waves, or go inside when the sun got too hot and read in the air-conditioning.

I look at the sad, little cabin. Sigh.

As I climb out of the car, my sandal crunches down where I step. I look down and know that going barefoot is out of the question. If the pieces of broken shells don't poke me, then the brown stickers in the weeds will.

For the first time, I start to wonder if Sergio brought me along because he hoped I'd be disappointed. He'd been to the beach with his high school friends twice and kept saying that going to the beach was no big deal. But this is all new for me.

Carmen and Sergio walk up the crooked porch. I take one more look at the cabin, hoping that they made a mistake.

Carmen opens the door and I can hear voices: "Carmen's here! Sergio's here! They're here! They're here!"

This is the place. It's no mistake.

I step inside, behind Carmen and Sergio. The house feels even hotter than outside. A mom and dad, brothers, and sisters, a house full of people talking at once, but not to me. I slide along the wall until I bump into this lumpy green chair. I'm stuck here for the next two days.

"What took you all so long?"

The question comes from a fat boy who's spread himself all over the green chair. I know his name is Frankie, and he is twelve. Carmen told me.

"The ferry had a long line," I tell Frankie.

He makes a hissing noise between his teeth, then says, "Dad, can we go to the beach now? Waiting for Carmen's so boring."

Suddenly, Carmen takes my hand and introduces me to her mother. Mrs. Sandoval catches me so tight in a hug, I can smell her breakfast. I feel so weird. Hugging people I barely know is what we always do in Mexico, but I don't think I'll ever get used to it.

"I'm so glad you came, Alicia." Mrs. Sandoval's face looks like Carmen's. I hope I'll like her just as much. She starts to smile, but something behind me catches her attention, and suddenly, she's frowning.

"Frankie! Turn off the TV. I told you to put the box by the door into the truck."

"I want to wear my bikini today. Why can't I?" says Carmen's little sister, Tita. She shoots up out of nowhere, tugging on her mother's arm. I met her a couple of weeks ago when Mom and I were shopping at the mall. Carmen told me Tita is eight.

"You going to burn yourself up on the first day? You put on your old suit and get one of Frankie's T-shirts too," Mrs. Sandoval answers.

"I hate wearing Frankie's T-shirts. They smell." Tita squeezes her face together like she's going to cry and stomps out of the room.

A sticky something splatters on my leg before I see the little, black-haired boy pushing between me and Mrs. Sandoval. A glob of jelly's stuck on me now.

"I want to go to the beach! Go to the beach now."

"This is Sammy," Carmen says. "He's four and he's a mess."

"Carmen, clean up Sammy." Mrs. Sandoval puts the boys arm into Carmen's hand, then says, "And where did your father go to?"

"Mama, check the ice chest. Do we have everything?"

A tall man with a thick black moustache had left, but now comes back through the door where Carmen takes Sammy. He gives me a stare. "Another daughter this week-end, eh? Named Alicia, right? Do you eat as much as your brother does?"

"No, sir," I say, getting more nervous by the minute about being a part of this family's vacation.

"Frankie, get out of that chair and start loading the truck. Sergio, help Frankie with the tent and make sure all six poles are there." Mr. Sandoval speaks up and everyone starts moving around.

But I'm not sure what I'm supposed to do. I want to help, but how? Where? I head towards Sergio, who's gone outside with Frankie.

I stand on the porch and watch Frankie do a hoppy-jumpy dance over the crunchy patches leading to a blue truck.

"Don't you have some shoes?" Sergio asks.

"Aw, stickers don't hurt me," Frankie says.

My brother shakes his head as if he thinks Frankie's a loser, then he sees me. "Well, don't just stand there, Alicia. Get our stuff out of the car. And go change."

His voice is bossy as always, but I am actually glad he told me to do something.

Carmen comes outside and asks Sergio for the keys, and both of us unpack the trunk.

I follow Carmen with my suitcase through the living room. She takes me through an L-shaped bedroom with two double beds, inside a kitchen that smells like *chile* and bacon, and onto a screen porch with six cots. Carmen tosses her gray duffel bag on one canvas cot, only to have it fade out in a cloud of dust.

"We always sleep out here. Because of the screen, they'll be no mosquitos," Carmen says.

There won't be any air-conditioning either, I think. My clothes are already stuck to my skin. I put my suitcase in the cot nearest the door. There's a small table by it, and I can spread my stuff out.

"I hope you have fun this weekend," Carmen says to me.

Before I answer, Mr. Sandoval shouts, "I'm leaving in five minutes. If you're not ready, you can just stay here!"

"Hurry, Alicia. Get your suit. There's always a line for the bathroom," Carmen says as she pulls her shiny blue bathing suit out of the front zippered compartment of her bag. She runs out of the room.

I wish I had time to sort through my stuff. I take my new purple-striped plastic bag out of the suitcase. The words, BEACH BAG, are printed in gold. It smells so clean. I start putting in my sunscreen lotion, my camera, my sandals, and my hat. Then I still have to shove my sunglasses, my favorite book, my towel, an extra change of clothes, and my little radio into it. The bag looks ready to explode. I dump it all out on the cot, ready to start again.

The others in the house call out to each other.

"Where is Sammy's red bucket?"

"Did you get the towels?"

"Don't forget your extra T-shirt."

"Who's hogging up the bathroom?"

Sergio shows up, and drops his duffel bag on a gray cot near Carmen's. "Aren't you ready yet?"

He's always so pushy! I make my own pig noise and stare at him. "You're not ready either!"

He laughs, which makes me even madder. Like nothing, he pulls his white muscle-shirt over his head. Then he unzips his bag, pulls out a torn green T-shirt that looks like a car ran over it, and puts that on over his jean cut-offs.

"I'm ready for the beach," he says with that old know-it-all face I hate.

I could hardly believe that Sergio was dressed that way for the beach. Mom would have killed him. I don't want to claim him.

Suddenly, Carmen yells, "Alicia, have you changed yet?"

I hate to leave my stuff spread out everywhere, but I can't help it. I grab my new bathing suit and run towards the bathroom, praying that Mr. Sandoval isn't going to leave to the beach without me.

Chapter Four
Jellyfish Girl

Carmen's dad has to win first prize for finding every rut, dip, and hole on the beach. For the tail end of this ride from the house to the beach, I just shut my eyes, trying to get ready for the next time I'll bounce around. Banging my elbows and knees, I get knocked off balance. I have lumps on my bumps by the time Mr. Sandoval stops the truck.

"Last one in smells like a squid!" Frankie crows.

The truck sways from side to side as heavy footsteps thump beside me. Frankie gallops off the truck bed. He's followed by quick, lighter steps. I guess Tita's followed him, because she doesn't want to smell like a squid either. I hear Carmen giggling, and Sergio grunting, but no footsteps. I guess they jumped off the side.

Finally, the person who smells like a squid opens her eyes.

I hear the roar of the ocean behind me. In front of me, I see hills of sand. Slowly, I crawl off the truck, and slide down the tailgate.

The sand is cool and soggy under my feet. I look down, watching my toes curl and wiggle. I bend down to touch the new sandy patterns my feet make. Rubbing sand between my fingers, it reminds me of the brown sugar my mother uses for cookies.

That thought makes me want to taste it, so I look over my shoulder. Nobody's watching. Like a lizard, my tongue shoots out for a quick lick.

"Yuck!" I spit out the taste. "Sand is sand."

I dust my hand off on my red and white bathing suit. My eyes start to follow the trails of tire tracks into the sand hills. The skinny green weeds and stalks of yellow grass poking out of the white sand hills remind me of Tío Chale's bald head.

Three sea gulls fly by. My eyes follow their path. I turn around, and for the first time face the ocean.

I am really HERE. I stare at the water. It's like it melts into the far away where the sky begins. The water rolls up and shoots out in big waves which grow smaller as they come closer to the sandy beach.

Frankie and Tita are already kicking water at each other. Sergio and Carmen are holding hands and walking by the edge. Little Sammy clutches a hand of his mother and one of his father, as he jumps over the lines of water washing onto the sand.

Everyone's enjoying the water but me!

The blue-gray water has white foam tops. The ocean looks different from any picture I've ever seen. I think about my camera, but shake my head. This is the time for me to know stuff for real.

As I walk, pieces of dry weeds sometimes prick my feet. I hop over a piece of wood with little clam shells stuck to it. I'm pretty close to the water when I see a blue plastic bubble shimmering in the sand. I make a quick detour in its direction.

As I stand over it, I notice the purple squiggles framing the blue object. It looks like a balloon. I bend down to see my first jellyfish. I saw a picture in one of my science books, and I read that even lying on the shore, it can give a painful sting. It amazes me to think that something so delicate and beautiful can be so dangerous.

"Alicia! Don't touch that!" Sergio yells.

From out of nowhere, Sergio's feet appear beside the jellyfish, and then, Carmen's smaller feet with ten red toenails.

"You think I'm stupid?" I tell Sergio. I put my hands on my hips, then stare into his black eyes. "It's a jellyfish. I'm not going to touch it!" I push my heels into the mushy sand and walk away.

Suddenly, I make a wild run into the ocean. I cry out as the cold water first hits me. Goose bumps pop out on my legs. I start jumping around, trying to get used to the wet, chilly skin. Salty drops splash my face, and I taste them on my tongue. It's a weird flavor, but not too bad.

My toes sink into the squishy bottom. I look down and laugh because I can see my feet, but I don't see a reflection of my self like I do when I swim in a pool.

Tita and Frankie start calling to me. I can see them further into the waves. The water is barely at their waists. Since I'm a pretty fair swimmer, I don't feel scared to walk out to where they're standing.

They tell me to turn my back on the bigger waves and let the water wash over me. The first one knocks me down, and I swallow a mouthful of water. Blegh! I wave my arms around, trying to get my balance. Frankie grabs my arm and yanks me up. But another wave hits us, and both of us go under the salty water.

I'm spitting out salty water, and Frankie's laughing harder. We finally get on our feet. By the third wave, I learn how to push my hips and back into the curve to help me keep my balance. My skin soaks up salt water like a sponge, and my long hair hangs around me like wet ropes. I laugh too, as we get hit again and again. Fighting the salty waves is a blast!

Soon Sergio and Carmen show up. Sergio's carrying a white board with him. It looks like the tip of a surfboard, but as I see it closer, it's made of styrofoam, like the Sandoval's spotted ice chest.

"Me first! Me first!" Tita calls out, and bounces in the water over to Sergio.

Sergio lays the foam surf board down on the water. Tita jumps forward, to lay her chest on the board. She grips it with her hands on both sides.

As the next wave comes, the movement sends Tita on a ride back to the shore. Two more waves take her to knee-deep water, then she stands up and starts half-walking, half-riding back to where we are.

"Let Alicia have a turn," Carmen says.

Tita passes the board over to me. I glance at Sergio, hoping he'll help me too.

But I see Sergio's got Carmen in a hug. He's saying something that makes her smile big. The last time I interrupted the love birds, Sergio bit my head off. I decide I can do this surf board stuff on my own.

"This'll be fun," I tell Tita and slide the board near my chest. I try to jump onto it the same way Tita did.

About the same time, a big wave flushes over us. Instead of riding the surf, the board completely flips over, and I go under. Instead of riding the wave, I'm swallowing it in big gulps. My eyes burn. I'm choking and coughing.

As quick as I can, I raise my head out of the water. I shove the hair out of my face, and see the surf board floating away with another wave.

"Get the surfboard!" Sergio yells.

I stand up, wiping my nose, which itches from all the salt water inside it. Frankie splashes after the riderless board. I look back at Sergio. Does he think that stupid board is more important than me? I could have been drowning!

"You okay, Alicia?" Carmen says.

When I look at her, she's laughing. I guess I can't blame her. I must have looked pretty funny flipping over in the waves.

"I feel like I just drank up the whole ocean," I say.

Frankie shows up with the surf board. "My turn!" he crows just as he jumps onto it. A big wave slaps us all off balance, and sends Frankie riding to the shore.

Again I push my wet hair out of my eyes, and spit out salt water. "I want to try the board again."

"Why don't you let Sergio hold you?" Tita says to me.

My eyebrows scrunch up when I look at Sergio.

"Sure, okay." Sergio shrugs, and then turns his eyes back to Carmen. "When do you want to take your turn, Baby?"

Carmen leans against Sergio's arm and whispers something in his ear. She giggles, he laughs. Then he kisses her lips.

"Oh gross!" Tita groans.

I agree. Kissing a jellyfish would be better than kissing Sergio.

There's a lot of splashing when Frankie returns, floating on the board, using his big arms to swim back to us.

"Okay, Sergio. Now hold the board for Alicia so she can get ready for the wave," Tita says.

I laugh at the way she bosses Sergio around.

"Okay, Alicia, let's go." He takes the board from Frankie, then moves next to me.

I give him a look, wondering if he'll really help me.

"I promise not to let you go until you're ready." Then he makes his sneaky laugh. Should I trust him?

"Hurry up!" Frankie says.

I slide in between Sergio's long brown arms. The board rests at my waist. Quickly, I jump up and balance my chest upon it.

"Here comes the wave. Are you ready?" His voice rumbles inside my ear.

He yells, "Hang on!" Suddenly, a strong wave shoots me forward.

I clutch both sides of the board. It's smashing my chest, but I don't care. I feel like a mermaid, sailing on that foam board. Just as I start to slow down, another wave comes and carries me further. Closer and closer, to the shore where Sammy is digging in the sand with a red shovel.

Then I hear everyone yelling behind me. Everyone's splashing and running. Tita's waving her arms and screaming. And I never thought someone as fat as Frankie could move so fast through the waves.

I slide off the board. "Ow, ow! Ouch!" My knees scratch the sandy ocean bottom. As I stand up, the waves barely cover my knees. Somebody's splashing me, and when I turn around, Carmen and Sergio have finished a run through the water too.

"What's wrong?" I ask, wondering what all the shouting and running meant.

"There was a jellyfish swimming in the waves." Carmen's laughing as she stops by me, but I see her brown eyes are bigger than usual. "You took off at just the right time, Alicia."

"Thanks for the ride, Sergio," I tell my brother.

"Put the board back in the truck, Alicia," he says, and puts his arm around Carmen's shoulder. "We'll swim later."

For once, I have to agree with my brother. Who wants to swim with a jellyfish?

Chapter Five
Sand and Jar

"Let's build a sand castle!" Tita suggests as we all meet up on the beach.

"I'll help you," I say. Making a sand castle was one thing I planned to do when I came to the beach. Besides, I wanted to give the jellyfish lots of time to get out of the piece of ocean where I'm swimming.

"Sammy's already got us started," Frankie says, and he leads the way to where his little brother sits digging in the sand.

"Sergio! Frankie! Come help me put up the tent!" Mr. Sandoval's deep voice makes everyone pay attention. Near the truck, he's got this green square laid out in the sand. He's carrying a hammer and some metal poles.

I look at Carmen. "What do we need a tent for? I thought we were sleeping at the cabin."

"It's for shade. The sun will be really hot soon. We'll get roasted without it," Carmen tells me. She goes off to help her father too.

I squint at the sun. Even though I'm wet, I can feel myself drying out pretty fast. My skin's brown, but I've been sunburned before. Having a place out of the sun seems like a good idea.

"Here, Alicia." Tita tosses a yellow plastic rake at my feet. She's kneeling in the sand by Sammy. "You can dig a moat around the castle."

I start scooping sand up, pressing my knees deeper into the scratchy sand. It sticks to my legs, my hands, and my bathing suit right away. Sammy's round cheeks are covered by it. Was he curious about the flavor of beach sand too? I smile at him and wonder what it must be like to have a little brother around.

Watching Tita shape mounds of sand, my brain starts to design a good moat. Sammy's little rake helps me dig out a rough plan. Then I start digging an L-shaped hole around Tita's castle. Sammy decides it's more fun to dump sand from his bucket into the long hole I've dug. He thinks its funny, but I don't.

"Why don't you put some sand here?" I ask him pointing to a spot away from the moat I'm digging.

"No. I build a castle."

"I know. But this is the moat. Like a river, you know? It will go around the castle."

Sammy shakes his head. "I build a castle here."

"Here, Sam. You dig here. You can help, Alicia." Tita starts to dig sand up in another spot with Sammy's red shovel. He had tossed it down when he picked up his bucket of sand to dump in my moat.

Tita hands the shovel to him and he starts digging instead of dumping. "Good boy, Sammy."

As Frankie shows up, I begin to think about how things would be if there were four kids in my family. Would I like it better with more brothers and sisters?

Frankie plants himself beside Sammy, lying down on his stomach, close to where Tita's crawling around.

"Move, Frankie. You're in my way," Tita says.

"I'm going to help Sammy," he replies.

"Go on, Frankie. You're too fat to fit here."

"Okay, okay." Frankie turns over on his back. "I need to work on a tan anyway." Then he extends his arms out to the side, laying one of them right in the wall of Tita's castle.

"Hey!" She grabs his arm and throws it up, but it comes down again, crumbling more of her sand wall.

"Frankie! You're messing everything up!"

"Hey! I can lay anywhere I want to."

Tita turns around. Her fingers start pinching and poking the rolls of fat on Frankie's bare brown chest and stomach.

He starts laughing, then crosses his arms across himself to block her tickling fingers. "Stop it! Stop it!"

"Make me," she says, starting to laugh herself.

Suddenly sand starts flying. Tita grabs sand from the remains of the castle walls and throws it at Frankie. He blocks her hand, though, and the sand hits Sammy's legs instead. Frankie grabs at the sand again, then Tita throws back. Before I know it, Sammy starts throwing sand at his brother and sister. I'm caught in the crossfire of a Sandoval Sand War!

47

Before I can decide which side to join, Sammy starts screaming because there's sand in his eyes. He rubs his eyes with sandy fingers, and starts crying louder and louder.

Mrs. Sandoval runs up, with Carmen and Sergio behind her. "What happened?" she asks, scooping a crying Sammy into her arms. She starts wiping his face with her white shirt.

"Tita did it," Frankie says at the same time Tita says, "Frankie started it first!"

"Frankie and Tita threw sand at me," Sammy cries.

Mrs. Sandoval gives her sandy kids a Mad-Mom look. Even poor little Sammy.

"What's wrong with you kids? Sergio and Alicia are going to think you all act no better than animals!" Mrs. Sandoval says all this in Spanish. It sounds just like something my Mom would say.

Mrs. Sandoval turns and walks off with Sammy, who's crying like a shark chewed his leg off. I think he's acting like a big baby. I decide a little brother would get on my nerves. And at least I only have to put up with Sergio, not three others, like Carmen does.

"What a sad, sad castle," Tita says, looking at me.

"Okay, okay. Let's get organized." Bossy old Sergio starts giving orders. "Frankie, you work on some towers. Tita, you do the sides and front. Alicia, keep digging the moat."

"And what are you and Carmen going to do?" I ask him.

"Supervise!"

They both say this at the same time, then start laughing like they've just told the funniest joke in the world.

I just roll my eyes, and start scratching at the itchy sand on my arms. My finger slides into something slimy. I notice the black spot on my arm. When I try to wipe it off with my finger, it smears into a black stripe.

"Yuck!" I say, making a face. "What's this black stuff?"

"It's tar," Tita says. "It's 'cause the oil ships leak, and the oil floats to the beach."

Frankie makes a laughing noise. "That's why I like black shorts." He's pounding a sand wall into place. "Black clothes won't show the tar."

I push up on my knees and start looking myself over. My eyes get bigger. Spots of tar dot the bottom of my new suit and the back of my legs. "Oh, my gosh. I've got this stuff all over me!"

"It's better to wear old clothes and then throw them away. I learned that last year during Spring Break." Sergio scoops up a handful of sand and lets it run through his fingers. He sits by Carmen, who is scraping a doorway through the one wall the sand war didn't destroy.

My face feels like I have a bad sunburn. "Sergio, why didn't you tell me? This is a new bathing suit."

He looks up at me. His eyebrows meet like a black worm is crawling across his nose. "I did say something. Last night when you were packing. You told me to get lost, remember?"

I feel like throwing a handful of sand at Sergio's stupid expression. Last night he had said, "What are you packing so much stuff for? Take old clothes like I do."

And I did tell him to get lost. But he never told me why he brought old clothes to the beach. He knows it's better to throw away old clothes than bring them home and listen to Mom yell. Why didn't he tell me?

"Don't worry, Alicia," Carmen says, patting my knee. "Any kind of oil will get it off. When we get back to the cabin, you can clean up."

I rest back on my heels and sigh. I'm stuck being a zebra until we get back. What'll I tell Mom? Can I blame all this on Sergio?

"Alicia, you didn't finish the moat," Tita says. "Every nice castle has a moat."

The castle in front of me still needs a lot of work. I grab the shovel and start digging again.

"Let's make something spectacular. Then I can take a picture of it," I say, trying to forget about the tar for now.

"Come on, Carmen, let's go for a walk," Sergio says, and he jumps up and sticks his hand down for Carmen to take. She smiles up at him, forgetting all about us, and stands up.

"Can I be in the picture with the castle?" Tita asks me.

I glance at Carmen and Sergio walking away, and then back at Tita. "Sure, you can be in the picture."

"Why would Alicia want your goofy face in her picture?" Frankie tells his sister.

I start to worry if another sand fight will start. At the same time, I notice Frankie's building up the wall his arm had smashed down.

"Why don't we let your dad take the picture," I say. "Then, we can all be in it. It's only fair, since we're all building the castle together."

"Oh, keep Frankie out of it. He's so ugly, he'll probably break the camera," Tita says, and moves out of Frankie's reach.

"And you're so skinny, Alicia's mom will look at the picture and think you're just a piece of drift wood," Frankie answers.

They continue to insult each other, and Frankie tells corny jokes. And we all laugh a lot.

We build this sand castle which doesn't look anything like the fancy castles I saw in my geography book. When it's finished though, I'm still happy. Since I helped build this crooked sand castle with uneven towers, I think it's beautiful.

Chapter Six
Beach Food

Building a castle is sticky, hot work. Sergio takes pictures of all of us behind the castle. Then Frankie, Tita, and I go into the shallow water to rinse the sand off our bodies.

"You think the jellyfish swam away?" I ask Frankie.

He squats down in the water, so the waves can wash over his shoulders. "What jellyfish?"

"The one from this morning," I say, bouncing down in the water to rinse off, then standing up again. "The one swimming in the water."

Frankie just laughs. "You always got to look out for jellyfish."

I look around where I'm standing. The water around me is knee deep. Then I feel something brush against my leg, then grab my ankle and give it a good shake.

I scream, jumping up. Frankie really starts laughing because he grabbed me underwater to scare me. I start laughing too. Usually I'm not a chicken.

Tita's laughing at us, then I see her point. "Look!"

Both Frankie and I turn around. I see a silver fish about eight inches long jump through the waves. And then another fish jumps up, wiggles through the air, and plops back into the waves.

"Oh wow! We need fishing poles!" I say to everyone.

"Naw, that's just a mullet." Frankie stands up. "You can't eat those. They're only good for cut bait."

I shrug my shoulders. A fish is a fish to me. I'd still like to catch one this week-end.

Mrs. Sandoval calls to us to come eat lunch. I suddenly feel real hungry. My stomach growls as I follow the others under the shade and smell the skinny sausages Mr. Sandoval's grilling on a short barbecue pit. Beside the brown sausages, he's got a foil tray piled with flour tortillas.

"Serve yourselves," Mrs. Sandoval says. She's sitting in a nylon folding chair, and pulls Sammy, who's wrapped in a towel, onto her lap. Sammy's holding a sausage wrapped in a napkin, and he's munching on it like he's pretty hungry too.

Mr. Sandoval puts a warm flour tortilla on my plate then spears a sausage from the grill and sets it in the tortilla.

I thank him, then move to the square folding table behind him to squeeze some mustard on my meat and grab a handful of chips from an open bag.

All of this reminds me of being on a picnic, except there aren't any ants. I like eating on the beach instead of going back to the cabin.

Sergio and Carmen take the other two folding chairs, so I sit on one of the two canvas stools near the ice chest.

I sit down, balance my plate on my legs, then roll the tortilla around my sausage. I take a small bite 'cause I know it'll be hot. I chew the tasty meat, but also, I'm crumbling something between my teeth. I take another bite and kind of chew slower, staring down at the sausage. Then I realize what I'm tasting. Sand. Maybe it's just my mind playing tricks. Even though I rinsed off, I still feel sandy, which isn't surprising, since the sand's in the salt water too. I can even feel it in the breeze cooling us under the tent.

"Alicia, you want a soda? Frankie, get Alicia a soda from the ice chest," Mr. Sandoval says.

I nod my head because I'm still chewing my crunchy sausage taco. It doesn't taste too bad if I don't think about the crunching.

Frankie pops the top on a can of soda and hands it to me.

"Thanks," I tell him and can't wait for the cold drink to wash the sand out of my mouth. When I take a swallow, the red soda tastes saltier than I remember. I take another drink, and still feel the sand and salt in my mouth. This is something I wasn't expecting, and I'm not sure what to think about it.

"Aw man!" Frankie groans loudly.

The others start laughing because Frankie's dropped his sausage in the sand. I smile, but I don't laugh. I know if I did that, I'd feel so embarrassed.

"Just wash it off in the ocean," Mrs. Sandoval says.

Frankie shrugs, picks up the sausage, and carries it between two fingers down towards the water. I can't believe it. I think I'd rather skip lunch that eat a sausage washed in salt water.

I watch Frankie bend over in the waves, wash off the sausage, then start munching on it. By the time he reaches the shade, he's finished eating it and goes to the barbecue pit for another.

"You want to do some fishing today?" Mr. Sandoval asks Frankie as the boy wraps a tortilla around two sausages. He doesn't drop anything this time.

Frankie nods as he takes a big bite. "Just you and me?" he says between chews.

"I usually catch the best fish," Carmen says. "Sergio and I can come too."

"What about Alicia?" Tita asks.

I look at Mr. Sandoval, hoping he'll let me come along.

Mr. Sandoval's moustache moves side to side as he stares at me. "Ever been fishing before, Alicia?"

I swallow, then nod. "Yes, sir. A couple of times, but I never caught anything."

"Sure you did, Alicia. At Tío Chale's pond. You caught that big goldfish, remember?" Sergio says, and he's grinning like a clown.

My face starts burning up. What will Carmen's family think if Sergio tells that story? Too late. Sergio loves to make me look stupid.

"Alicia was five," he says. "And we were visiting my uncle's ranch near Puebla. He has this rock pond in the middle of his patio. Some goldfish about this big live in it." Sergio uses his hands to show the fish are about the size of the mullet I saw in the waves.

"Well one afternoon, while everyone else is taking a siesta, Alicia decides she's going to go fishing. She finds a stick and some string, and jumps into the pond, and tries to tie up a fish."

"I didn't have any hooks!" I say to Carmen's family, just like I had told everyone at Tío's house that day. "And Tío said he felt like eating fish for supper that night."

"You mean Alicia caught a fish with her hands?" Tita's brown eyes are big and round as she looks from Sergio to me.

Sergio's laughing more, and so are the others. "She grabbed the fish and stuck it under her arm pit, trying to tie it onto the string. That's how my uncle found her."

I only wish I had a story about Sergio and a fish to tell everyone. I want to crawl into a shell like a hermit crab.

"You know, Alicia? That's a cool story," Frankie says. "I tried to catch a flounder once, but it slipped out of my hands."

"Well, unless you got arms like an octopus, you won't be able to catch fish with your hands off a pier," Mr. Sandoval says. He gives me a friendly wink before he asks, "Alicia, do you think you could use a pole and hook for fishing today?"

I finally smile. "Sure, Mr. Sandoval." It seems like he'll take me fishing with everyone else after all.

"Anybody want some cookies?" Mrs. Sandoval asks, and soon a bag of homemade chocolate chip cookies gets passed around.

The one I take is a fat, round one exploding with chocolate chips. I bite into it, only to taste some invisible frosting. It's still delicious, but there's a sandy, salty flavor too. I'm getting used to it.

After lunch I decide that washing a sausage in the ocean before eating it isn't as yucky as I first thought. When you're eating on the beach, a little extra salt water doesn't make much difference.

Another hour in the water, then we pack up the truck and head back to the cottage to leave Mrs. Sandoval and Sammy to siesta while the rest of us go fishing. Tita says it's too hot and she will stay with her mother. Mr. Sandoval and Frankie take time to fix a small ice chest with fresh ice and sodas. Carmen's bathing Sammy, and that leaves Sergio and me outside. Waiting.

"Why don't you stay here with Tita?" Sergio says as I sit on the crooked porch smearing sunscreen on my arms.

"Mr. Sandoval said I could come fishing," I tell him, wishing Sergio would stay here with Tita instead.

"It'll be hot. There's no bathroom. Or shade. We'll be out fishing all afternoon. I'm not taking my car. If you get tired, too bad. You'll be stuck out there until everyone else wants to stop fishing."

I say nothing at first. I want to fish, and Sergio can't change my mind. Finally, I stand up and twist the cap of the sunscreen bottle very tight, pretending it is Sergio's neck. "I'm going to get my hat and go to the bathroom. Then I'll be ready."

"Hey! Let me have that sunscreen lotion!" he says as I turn to go inside the yellow house.

I rub my greasy hands all over the bottle, then toss it at him. I hear it thump on the porch just before the screen door slams behind me.

Chapter Seven
Shrimp Coats or Squid?

After a quick stop to put gas in the truck and buy some bait, Mr. Sandoval drives down a busy road. It takes us straight to the spot on the beach where the long pier stands.

The fishing pier's made of the same black wood poles and boards like most of the docks and bridges. We walk up this warped ramp on the sandy beach that leads up to the pier extending out into the water. I'm glad to see railings on both sides to keep us from falling off.

At the window of a white building that sells sodas and bait, Mr. Sandoval pays a dollar for each of us to fish. Mr. Sandoval tells Sergio to carry the ice chest. Carmen's got the poles. I have a green tackle box, and Frankie's finishing up the bag of cookies I thought we were all going to share later.

The pier itself seems to go out a long way. As we walk along, I'm both scared and excited to see the water through the tiny cracks between the boards. Stopping to look over the side of the pier, I wonder how deep the water would be if a big fish pulled me in.

Although it's the hot part of the afternoon, there are more than a dozen people fishing. There's one woman wearing a man's work shirt and rolled up jeans. She smiles at us. She looks older than my great-grandmother. Some boys about Tita's age are with their father. The boys sit on a stiff, red ice chest as they fish. I'm watching the others until Mr. Sandoval stops and says, "Let's fish here."

Sergio drops the ice chest down. It almost smashes my foot. I put down the tackle box, then look over the railing.

"Sergio and I will fish further down," Carmen says. "I don't want to be around Frankie when he starts casting."

"Yeah, right," he says, crunching up the empty cookie bag. "I'm not the one who keeps reeling in sea weed or gets my hook caught on the pier." He shoots the wadded bag into a rusty trash can close by.

Sergio takes one of the poles from Carmen. He leans a small red rod against the pier railing. It fits just perfectly into a notch somebody cut into the wood. "Here, Alicia. Use this pole."

I look up. Between Sergio's black sunglasses and his blue baseball cap, I can't see his expression. "I didn't know you brought any fishing poles."

"Well, you don't know everything, do you, Genius?" Sergio turns to follow Carmen further down the pier.

Good old Sergio. Just as I think he's doing something nice, he opens his mouth and ruins everything.

I watch as Mr. Sandoval opens the green plastic tackle box. There are different little boxes on the top tray. I see many sizes of hooks and metal weights. He selects a small hook and weight, and ties them on the end of the clear line of my fishing pole. Frankie's putting two hooks on his line and a medium size weight.

"We need some squid," Carmen says, returning to our spot.

I never thought about the bait. And this morning, when Frankie yelled, "Last one in smells like a squid," I didn't know what he meant.

I learn a lot watching Carmen take a small cardboard box from the ice chest. It looks like one of those boxes that Chinese food comes in. She puts the box on the railing and opens it. She pulls out a pinkish-white glob of something. Even if I didn't see the two black eyes sticking out, and the stringy legs, I would know it was a fish just by the smell. Carmen lays it on the railing. Her father's busy fixing his own pole, and she borrows the knife hanging from the case on his belt. I watch her slice the squid into small pieces.

Slowly, I touch a piece of squid. It feels slimy, but smooth. It reminds me of the fatty white stuff my mother slices off meat before she cooks it. It doesn't look delicious to me, but I hope the fish think so.

I really want to catch a fish today.

"I like to use squid," Carmen says. "It stays on my hook longer."

"Maybe I'll use squid too." I nod like I know what I'm talking about.

Another fishy smell makes me turn in Frankie's direction. He's opened up another carton of bait. From the white box, he pulls out a gray colored shrimp. I've eaten boiled shrimp at seafood restaurants before, but never saw anyone slide a hook inside and around a shrimp. When Frankie's done, it looks as if his two hooks are wearing shrimp coats.

Carmen walks off with her chopped up squid, so I decide to use shrimp for bait. I stick my hand inside the white carton, and feel a tangle of cold shrimp bodies. The shells are hard, not like when they're boiled. I grab one out, and find my hook.

Remembering what I saw Frankie do, I put the point of the hook just below the head. I curve the body around until my hook wears a shrimp coat too.

Mr. Sandoval's hand presses on my shoulder. "You're doing fine, Alicia." He helps me position the fishing pole over the railing so that my hook and bait are dangling above the water.

"Now, press this trigger right here and drop your hook straight down," he says, showing me a white button.

After I see Frankie cast his line further out into the ocean, I ask Mr. Sandoval, "Will I catch anything so close to the pier?"

"Sure you can." He smiles at me, then moves over to fish with his long, blue rod and shiny, silver reel.

Well, I push the button. My fishing line makes a "zing" sound. I watch my shrimp sink into the ocean close to a telephone pole that supports the pier. Then I watch the waves slap against the pole. A crust of green stuff and some tiny shells are stuck to it. Huh, they never wash off.

The water moves my fishing line along, sometimes making it invisible because it's clear. A slight tug catches my attention. I look down and feel the pull whenever the waves come against the pier. I know, then, it's no fish.

Sigh. I let my eyes follow the ocean out until water melts into the sky. I wonder how it would be to sit in a boat and sail out as far as my eyes see. Even further. I wonder what the world looks like where the ocean ends.

I begin to dream about far away places and my adventures as a sailor.

"Have you caught anything yet?"

I jump a little when I hear Sergio's voice. My hands tighten around the pole. "No!"

"Have you checked to see if the bait's still there?" he says.

I blink at him. He just shows me his teeth.

"Reel it up, Alicia. Sometimes a crab eats the bait, or if you didn't hook it on right, a fish can snatch it off without you feeling it."

"You've only been to the beach a couple of times," I say. He acts like such a know-it-all. And Sergio's never brought home a fish he caught himself. "When did you learn so much about fishing at the coast?"

"I have a good teacher," he says, before he grabs a handful of shrimp from the carton. He goes back to his place by Carmen.

I ignore Sergio to look over the side of the pier and start reeling. Sure enough, the shrimp coat's been stolen off my hook. As I bring my line up, I notice Mr. Sandoval is cutting up another squid. I ask him for a piece.

"Did you feel anything take your bait?" he asks me.

"I felt a little pull, but I thought it was only the ocean making my line move," I tell him, feeling very dumb.

"Tricky fish or crabs, I bet. Just keep trying," he says, and helps me put squid on my hook.

Just before I'm about to drop my line again, I hear Frankie call out, "I got one."

After I lean my pole inside a notch, I walk over to him. He brings his line around. A silver-white fish dangles from the top hook.

Frankie holds his fishing pole between his legs. Then he gets a hand around the fish.

"Is it big enough to keep?" I ask him.

"Sure." His big fingers cover the top fins. With his other hand, he slides the hook back and forth in the fish's pink mouth until he unhooks it.

I follow Frankie back to his father, who opens the door on a flat wire basket that's attached to a long rope. Once the fish is inside, Mr. Sandoval ties the rope to the pier and drops the basket into the ocean.

"Okay, squid," I grumble as I go back to my pole. "Let's catch the next fish." I drop my fishing line into the ocean. I make myself stop dreaming and pay attention to the feel of my pole.

Any time I feel something, I reel in my line. In the next hour, I must reel in my line fifty times. That slimy squid still hangs off the hook each time.

In the meantime, Carmen's caught three fish, but only keeps one. Then she gives a loud cheer when Sergio catches one.

I'm inspecting my squid at the time. I can't see even a chew mark. I decide to go look at my brother's fish.

Sergio's got his pole in one hand. The other holds his line. At the end of the hook is one of the ugliest fish I've ever seen. It's a gray fish with a white stomach. These long, skinny things, like rubber whiskers, come out both sides of its head.

"What kind of fish is that?" I ask.

"Aw, it's just a hardhead," Frankie says, coming up behind me.

"Can you eat it?" I ask, but know I wouldn't want to.

Frankie laughs. "Even the fish don't want to eat a hardhead. Unless they're really hard up. Get it?"

Corny, but I laugh anyway.

"Sergio, can you get it off the hook?" Mr. Sandoval calls. He's the only one who's still fishing right now.

"Be careful," Carmen says. "Make sure you hold the fins down."

"I know what I'm doing," Sergio says as he hands Carmen his pole. He uses both hands to unhook the fish.

His long fingers look very brown against the fish's white gills. He slides his fingers down, over the stiff fins. The hook makes a gross crackling sound as Sergio jerks it around the fish's mouth. Finally, he rips the hook loose. Poor fish!

"Now what?" I say.

"You want it for a souvenir?" Sergio shoves the fish near my face. I hop back. He gives a big laugh, then tosses the fish over the side of the pier.

I can catch something better than a hardhead, I think, turning away to go back to my own fishing pole.

"Sergio got a hardhead, eh?" Mr. Sandoval says to me.

"Is it really called a hardhead?" I ask him.

He laughs, a nice friendly sound that helps me like Carmen's dad a lot. "It's really called a salt water catfish, but most people I know call it a hardhead," he says. "The Gulf's full of them."

I nod, and wipe the sweat off my nose. Even though I'm wearing my favorite cap and a T-shirt over my bathing suit, I can feel the sun baking me like an *empanada*. I stop to put on more sunscreen lotion and tell myself that this fishing stuff is a lot harder than it looks.

Chapter Eight
Fisherwoman

"Want a soda?"

"Yes." I barely look at Sergio because I'm focused on fish.

I hear the can open, then Sergio rests it on the pier railing beside a chopped up squid.

"Alicia, nobody said you *had* to catch a fish, you know." He leans his elbow on the railing, his body turned towards me.

"I want to catch a fish."

"Aren't you hot? We've been out here two hours." Sergio clears out his throat, then spits into the ocean.

"That's gross. Go spit somewhere else. I'm trying to catch a fish." My eyes burn as I look at him. I can't tell if he's giving me a dirty look because of his dark sunglasses.

Sergio mutters something and the only word I understand is "crazy." I just ignore him and keep fishing. He finally walks off.

Just as I'm reaching for the can of soda, the fishing pole shakes in my hand. I feel a pull, so I jerk the pole up and back, like I saw Frankie do when he caught his second fish.

The line tugs back. I start reeling, but whatever is on the hook doesn't want to come in. I see my pole bending down, and once again, I pull up and back.

"Sergio!" I call out. My heart seems to be doing wheelies inside my chest. My hands shake. Sweat slides into my eyes. "Sergio!"

"Come on, Alicia! Bring it in!" Frankie's voice calls.

I don't look anywhere but at the salty ocean. My pole's curving down as if it's pointing at my fish.

"Reel it in," Sergio's calling. Suddenly, he's beside me.

"Let me do it!"

"No! It's mine!" I jerk away from Sergio's shadow as the line tugs me forward again.

Then, there's Carmen's voice telling me to take it slow. Pull back. Reel again. At least she's not trying to take my pole away.

Frankie's come over now. He's leaning over the side of the pier shouting, "I can see it. It looks like a good one. Come on, Alicia. Reel it in."

Suddenly, it's over. The pulling stops. My fishing line wiggles in the breeze. As I reel it in, I can see the naked hook. It's been in and out of the water so often, I don't even remember if I put squid or shrimp on it. A sinking feeling drags my stomach down to my toes. I bet all the fish are laughing. They're all getting a free lunch today, thanks to me.

"The one that got away," Sergio says, and pats me on the head.

"Get lost," I tell him, reeling in my line to try again.

"Too bad, Alicia. Maybe next time," Mr. Sandoval says from where he's been fishing. Even he has already caught two fish.

"Can't we call it a day?" Sergio asks Carmen. They are standing behind me as I hook a shrimp and prepare to lower it into the ocean. "I'd love a shower and some air-conditioning. Wouldn't you?"

"Sounds good to me," she says.

"I'm hungry," Frankie says.

I push the button and let my hook fall into the ocean. When Mr. Sandoval says it's time to go, I'll stop. Not 'til then.

I keep my back to the others, looking into the ocean. I think about that old movie

Dad and I watched one night. This old fisherman, who looks older than the Alamo, sits in a little boat waiting for one fish. Finally, he catches it, and there's a big fight. He reels it in and it's as big as his boat.

I slap a mosquito biting my leg. I don't want a fish the size of a boat. Even if I caught a hardhead like Sergio, at least I could say, "I caught a fish at the beach."

A smile sneaks up to my lips. Now I know how "fish stories" get started. If I caught an ugly fish like Sergio's, I'd probably make up lies as I told the story.

Frankie goes back to fishing. Carmen and Sergio go for a walk down the pier. I keep feeling tugs, reel in my line and put new bait on the hook.

Some time later, Mr. Sandoval calls over to Frankie and me. "We're down to the last couple of shrimp. We'll go when we're out, okay?"

My teeth start chewing on my lips. They feel cracked and dry from being in the hot, salty air all afternoon. Actually, it doesn't feel as hot as when we first got here. I look up and around. I guess it must be about four or five by now. My growling stomach tells me it needs more than a can of soda or soon the grumbling will get louder.

The pole shakes in my hand. I feel a sharp tug. I jerk up and back. This time, I feel the jerk again. A steady pull curves the tip of the pole downward.

This time, I don't call out to the others. My teeth grind together as I tell myself to stay calm. I reel in slowly, pull back, then reel in again. My fish is a fighter, but so am I.

We get into a tug of war, but I take things slowly. I want to wear him out. He yanks, but I hang on. I pull back again.

"I want you." I'm talking to a dumb fish. "You're mine. Now stop fighting. I'm going to win this time."

Mr. Sandoval is standing beside me, so I say no more. I don't want him to think I'm nuts.

I keep reeling. I pull back, then reel again. I glance down and see a silver fish wiggling just below the surface of the water. My whole body feels like a rubber band that's stretched too far.

"You got him, Alicia," Mr. Sandoval says to me. His voice is quiet. "Just reel him in."

As the fish rises above the water, my pole bounces up and down with the shakes and wiggles. That fish is determined to keep fighting until the end. As my hook and the fish reach the bottom of the pier, Mr. Sandoval reaches over to take my line in his hands. Even though I keep reeling, he pulls the fish over the railing.

I stare at a reddish-silver fish with blue-gray eyes. It's about a foot long. I remember that goldfish at Tío Chale's. My face feels like there's a spotlight on it.

"Can I eat it?"

"Let's gut it and cook it first, Alicia. Then you can eat it, okay?" Mr. Sandoval's shaking his head, laughing at me.

I laugh with him. It's nice to have a fish I can eat, but more than anything, I'm just glad to see this fish flopping on the pier instead of swimming in the ocean.

"Look, Frankie. I caught a fish!"

Frankie reels in his line. By the time he reaches us, Mr. Sandoval's wiggled my hook out of the fish's mouth. With his thumb and first finger, he's got the fish by the gills. It's stopped wiggling now. I guess that fish decided the fight is over. I won!

"Nice fish, Alicia." Frankie smiles at me, and thumps my shoulder. "We'll have a great fish barbecue tonight."

Mr. Sandoval tells Frankie to start packing up. Frankie and I toss the last shrimp and some squid guts up to a pair of sea gulls. Then I follow Mr. Sandoval and Frankie down the pier to a wooden tray with water faucets on each end. Sergio and Carmen show up just before Mr. Sandoval gives me a lesson in gutting and cleaning fish.

"That's a better fish than Sergio caught," Carmen says.

"That mullet is a better fish than Sergio caught," Frankie says, pointing to a dead fish someone left by the faucet.

I just laugh at all the jokes about Sergio's hardhead fish. It feels great to do something better than smarty old Sergio, even just for today.

Things get stinky and sticky as I learn to gut fish. I tell Mr. Sandoval that I'll do my own. Seems to me, it's all part of being a fisherman. No, fisherwoman.

I like the way fisherwoman sounds. I like the way it feels.

And I just can't wait to hear Sergio tell *his* fish story. I have one that is even better.

Chapter Nine

Two of a Kind

I sit down on the cement steps of the cottage. Carefully, I balance a paper plate on my knees. I sigh as the moisture from the cold triangle of watermelon soaks through the plate to cool my sunburned skin. After the morning on the beach and three hours on the pier, I feel more barbecued than the fish I ate for supper.

The sun's been down a while, but the skies are pretty to watch. Grayish purple skies with stripes of lavender and orange. I glance over at Frankie, who probably hasn't noticed and probably doesn't care.

He sits in a nylon chair catty-corner to the porch. His fat cheeks hide behind a smile-shaped watermelon slice he's holding between his two hands. His brown eyes look up a second to meet mine, but then they lower. Frankie chomps his way through the watermelon with noisy slurps and sucking sounds.

I use my plastic knife and fork to slice a bite-size piece from my watermelon, then slide it into my mouth. I chew and swallow, then sigh again. The watermelon's started to wash the sand out of my mouth for the first time all day.

Frankie lowers his watermelon. The pink juice runs down his chin. Stuffing fruit into the pocket of his cheek, he says, "Tastes great, doesn't it?"

"You want a napkin?" I ask, reaching for the extra paper towel I stuck into my shorts' pocket. He shakes his head and returns to his feast. I use the napkin instead.

Soon, he starts spitting out black seeds on the sidewalk near his bare feet. I can't help but notice the smudges of tar left on his toes.

After fishing, I try to get the tar off of me. Because it smells good, I use baby oil on a tissue to scrub off the tar. It doesn't do a good job. Then I follow Carmen's example and use the cooking oil. I am covered by a sandy slime that makes me feel awful.

I rub and rub until I am spot free. Thanks to the rough rag, the sand, and the sunburn, I am very red and sore by the time I get my turn in the shower.

My bathing suit's a sadder story. I scrub it and scrub it, but some stains are permanent. I decide to just wear the same suit tomorrow and not ruin any other clothes. As I shower and scrub off the slimy, greasy feeling, and wash out my hair, I plan to come to the beach again and be like Sergio: bring clothes I can throw away. Or I'll be like Frankie and wear black.

As Frankie sits with me now, eating his watermelon down to the rind, I wish I could be more like him. Nothing seems to bother him. I'm enjoying the watermelon bit by bit, but he just gobbles it up. Like everything else, Frankie grabs his fun in big pieces and doesn't worry over little things.

Soon he tosses the rind into a bumped-up can by the porch. He grabs the bottom of his baggy blue T-shirt and wipes his chin.

"Know what I like best about the coast?" he says. "No one cares if you're in old clothes and bare feet. And my mother never yells, 'Don't get dirty.'"

I chew on my lip as I think about Mom's reaction to the coast. She'd probably hate the taste of sand in her food. The messy black tar streaks up clothes and towels. The drinking water tastes different. Mom would be so busy cleaning and boiling, she'd never enjoy splashing in the waves or building piles in the sand.

I remember Mrs. Sandoval wading into the salty water to rinse the big knife and fork used to barbecue sausages. My mother would never do that. If Mom knew Sergio wiped squid guts on his clothes, she'd never let him into the house until he scrubbed himself with cleanser.

"What's so funny?" Frankie asks.

I realize I have a smile on my face. "I was thinking about the differences between your mom and mine," I tell Frankie.

"Yeah?" He leans back in the chair, scratching his flabby stomach. "Does your mom like the coast?"

I just laugh. "I think she'd hate this place. My mom wouldn't be happy until she swept all the sand off the beach."

Frankie's brown face opens up with big eyes and a grin. "That would take a giant-size broom."

"Maybe so, but my mom wouldn't stop 'til she finished."

"And you're just like her," he says with a laugh.

"What are you talking about?" I look at him like he said the dumbest thing I ever heard.

"You stood on the pier in the hot sun for three hours. You didn't want to leave until you caught a fish. You didn't even care when Sergio started complaining about how hot he was."

I'm used to Sergio only thinking of himself, but I hate to think I acted no better this afternoon. I hope I didn't spoil everything just because I wanted to catch a fish. "Do you think I made your dad angry?"

"Naw! Dad loves fishing. He could have stayed on the pier all night."

I feel better. I didn't want to act like a brat after Mr. Sandoval had been so nice.

"And once Dad taught you how to gut fish, you went crazy cleaning them all. Even the mullet by the faucet!" Frankie laughs again. "I've never seen anyone gut a mullet before."

I shrug my sunburned shoulders and pretend I knew what I was doing. "I just wanted the extra practice on gutting fish."

"Well, it was the cleanest bait on the pier!"

I laugh too. Mom would have approved of cleaning the bait and washing it before sticking it on a hook. The fish don't care, but Mom sure would.

Sitting back against the porch railing, I relax and enjoy thinking about my day. There are so many new feelings and tastes and sights and sounds and smells. My head needs more time to go through everything.

The screen door of the cabin squeaks behind me.

"Daddy says he'll take us to the channel park," Tita says. "Sammy wants to watch the boats. Alicia, do you want to come?"

My body's clean of tar, salt and sand. There's no more salty taste in my mouth. Why should I go back to the ocean when I can stay here?

"Sure, Tita! I want to come," I tell her without another thought.

It's almost dark when Mr. Sandoval drives us down the same main road that Sergio drove through earlier this morning. Near the ferry, there's a small park I hadn't noticed before. There are picnic tables, a swing set, a metal jungle gym, and a stone tower to climb and look out on the channel.

Mr. Sandoval says hello to an old man sitting on a bench, and they start talking in Spanish about the fishing. Sergio and Carmen take Sammy over to the swings. Me, Frankie, and Tita climb the tower. After three levels of stairs, we get up the platform and look around.

In the water, the ferry lights sparkle and dance. We see a big oil tanker pass through on its way out of the channel. All the ferries stop and let it pass.

As close as we are to the boats, the horns sounds as if they are far off. I guess the salty breezes carry the noises away from us.

I look up into the blue-black sky and see twinkles of stars and a white half moon. Once again, I think about the way the ocean and sky blend together. I feel small, yet safe and strong.

"This is all so pretty." I chew on my tongue after I say this. The words come out of my mouth before I think about how sappy I might sound.

"You know what I like best?" Frankie says, his chubby face raised up to the sky. "The beach at sunrise. That's really pretty."

I look at Frankie, a little surprised by a boy calling a sunrise "pretty." He's still looking at the sky. And I start to think that maybe I should go see the beach at sunrise for myself.

Tita and Frankie go back down, but I stay up there and watch the water and boats, not really thinking; just bringing everything I see inside of me.

"What are you thinking about?" Carmen says.

I never even heard her walk up the steps. I'm glad she's here now. She always makes me feel like my thoughts are important.

Before I can say anything, Sergio has clumped up the steps. He is breathing like he just ran around the park ten times.

Carmen giggles, and they start doing that kissing stuff. I look down to see Frankie and Tita climbing the jungle gym with Sammy. I think I should go down there and get away from the sounds of two people sucking their faces off, but I don't. I just move into the corner and try to ignore them.

Finally, Carmen comes again to the place where I'm standing. Unfortunately, she brings Sergio with her.

"Do you like the ocean, Alicia?" she asks me.

I love it. The ocean is the biggest thing I know. It's full of surprising creatures. It's salty and thick, and moves around all by itself. I love swimming in it, fishing in it, and I could come back again and again.

To Carmen, I just nod my head. I can't tell her anything about my feelings with Sergio around to hear them. I know he'd just laugh.

"Every summer since I was a baby, we've come here, " Carmen says. "I never get tired of it." When she gives a sigh, I know she understands my silence. "The view tonight is so beautiful, isn't it?"

"I wish we could stay here all night and watch the sun come up," Sergio says.

I turn, looking over my shoulder at Sergio. He's leaning against the short tower wall, his body turned towards the ocean. Something about his face looks different, as if maybe, by some miracle, he's got a heart that actually works like one.

"Why can't we come back at sunrise?" I ask. "Couldn't we, Sergio? Couldn't we come back—early in the morning—and watch the sun come up? All of us?" I add, just in case he takes my idea and keeps it for himself.

"I guess we could," he says, but his voice sounds as if it's working by itself. Is he really thinking about his words or just talking?

"I want to come too," I tell Sergio, meaning every word I say. "I want to see the beach at sunrise. You'll bring me too, won't you, Sergio?"

"Sure," he says, with a shrug.

"Promise? Sergio, do you promise? You'll take me in the morning?"

Finally he turns towards me, and that old growly look is back on his face. "Would you quit bugging me? I said I'd take you, didn't I?"

"Yes, you did." I answer very calmly, feeling like I am just as big as he is. After all, today I caught a better fish. I give my brother a smile, then turn back to stare at the ocean.

I can hardly wait for tomorrow, even though I never want this day to end.

Chapter Ten
Sunrise

My ears pick up the sound of crickets and a bird's cry. A smell of smoked fish hangs in the air. My eyes open. The bare wooden boards of the ceiling look unfamiliar. I move my body, and the scratchy stiff cot reminds me I'm far from home.

I get up on one elbow and look around. I blink a couple of times and wonder if the world turned to black and white while I was asleep. Across the small room, Tita's fluffy black hair falls over the pillow towards the floor. Her body's snuggled under a white sheet. It reminds me of a cocoon.

Not far from Tita, Frankie's dark chest rises and falls as he snores. Near the porch door is Sergio's cot. He lies on his back, his arm above his head. He has no sheet on, just jean cut-offs and a black tank top.

In the last cot, Carmen sleeps. Her white t-shirt's like a ghost against her tanned skin. A dark blanket covers her hips and legs.

I turn to look outside the screen porch. Above the next cabin, the sky's a weak blue. Thin grayish-green clouds look like smoke. I guess it's just before sunrise.

My heart seems to awaken. Excitement makes it beat stronger. Sergio said he would take me to see the beach at sunrise. I want to take pictures of the morning sun rising above the ocean. With those pictures, I can treasure the sunrise again and again; even when I sit inside the pink walls of my bedroom.

I hear a groan and quickly turn my face towards the noise. Sergio's moving in his cot. He's flipped on his side, and I see him reach out to stroke Carmen's black hair.

"Sergio!" I whisper.

I almost laugh as he nearly jumps above his cot.

"Sergio, can we go to the beach now?"

"Go to the beach? Are you nuts?" His hoarse whisper shoots across the room. He's turned on his stomach. I can barely see his face.

Carmen raises up on one elbow. "What's wrong?"

I sit up, hugging my knees to my chest. "Sergio, you promised you'd take me to the beach. I want to take pictures of the sunrise."

I'm ready to fight Sergio for this one favor, but I don't want to awaken the others. I hear Carmen whisper something to Sergio. I'm straining my ears, trying to listen.

Then I see Sergio sit up in his cot. Carmen's blanket flies back as she sits up. I know that Carmen's come to my rescue again. We're all going to the beach. I slide my sheet down my legs. Sergio better wait long enough for me to change out of my pajamas.

Carmen's standing by her cot, finger-combing her curly hair. She pulls her white T-shirt down over her shorts.

"Wait for me!" I whisper, wishing I had slept in my clothes like everyone else.

"No." Sergio's whisper stops me cold.

I sit on my cot, my toes barely touching the cement floor. "But it will only take me a second to change, Sergio."

He's standing at the end of my cot, his hands on his hips. "You stay here. I'll take your pictures. Where's your camera?"

As he comes closer, my heart seems to be pounding inside my ears. "But Sergio, I want to see the sunrise for myself."

"After the pictures come back to Photo-World, you can see the sunrise for yourself." He grunts. "We need to leave before everyone else wakes up."

"Can't I go too?" I look at Carmen, who shows up by Sergio. She always helps me when Sergio gets like this.

"We'll take good pictures," she says. "I promise, Alicia." Then she pats my head like I'm a puppy or something.

I jerk away from her hand as I do some quick thinking. If Carmen's on Sergio's side, maybe they want time alone without tag-a-longs.

"Look, I won't bother you two," I whisper. "Leave me at the pier, then come back for me later."

I think it's a great idea, but Sergio doesn't pay attention. He goes through my stuff on the little table by my cot until he finds my camera.

"If anyone wakes up, tell them we went to do a little fishing," Sergio whispers. He gives me a wink, then a sneaky smile.

My brother's pretty stupid if he thinks I'm going to tell anyone that lie. I sock my fist into the pillow instead of Sergio's face.

The two of them slip out the back porch door. I hear his car drive off.

I huff out a sigh and lay down on the cot. All I can do is wish for a sand crab to climb into Sergio's cut-offs. Give him a pinch he'll never forget. I start to imagine such an adventure for my brother. Soon I plot other stories: "Sea Creatures versus Sergio!" By the time the back porch begins to brighten with the sunrise, Sergio has been kidnapped by a family of crabs, stung by a giant jellyfish, and attacked by a man-eating HARD-HEAD. Each episode has Sergio begging for my help, but I turn away and say, "No, I'm going to take pictures of the sunrise." I leave him to battle alone. Too bad.

When I smell coffee, I figure Carmen's parents are awake, and it's time to get up.

"Morning, Alicia. Did the sea gulls wake you up?" Mrs. Sandoval asks when I come into the kitchen.

"I usually wake up early," I tell her, then take a seat by Mr. Sandoval, who's drinking a cup of coffee.

We talk about my school, my parents, and my uncle's ranch. Then Sammy wakes up and hangs all over Mrs. Sandoval, who's trying to scramble some eggs for breakfast.

So I ask Sammy to show me all the shells he found on the beach. He leaves his mom alone and takes my hand to pull me into the living room.

We're counting his shells when Carmen and Sergio come through the front door. I pretend like I'm really busy with Sammy, so they won't see I'm trying not to laugh. I had latched the back screen door, so they would have to come through the front.

Sergio says nothing as he walks through. His face looks angry, but I ignore him. Carmen sits on the sofa behind Sammy and me.

I feel her stroke my head, but I don't pull away.

"We only got a few pictures, Alicia. The mosquitos were awful. Even inside the car."

Once she leaves, I laugh to myself. Sergio versus the mosquitos. Not as good as a man-eating hardhead, but it'll do.

I still feel mad I couldn't see the sunrise myself, but I know it would be dumb to try and stay mad about it all day. I have better things to do. I promised myself Sergio would not spoil this trip and I mean it. Just the same, I'm glad a few mosquitos spoiled his fun this morning.

Sammy and I return to the kitchen when Mrs. Sandoval calls us. She's made tacos of scrambled eggs, *chorizo*, and bacon.

After breakfast I climb into a stiff, sticky suit spotted with tar, yet I can't wait to get back to the beach.

Once again, Mr. Sandoval drives several lumpy miles on the sand. This time, I prepare myself by using the foam board to kneel upon. I put my beach towel like a pillow between me and the truck.

As we drive along, I watch sea gulls picking at the sand. A family of four is setting up an orange tent. Two old ladies walk near the water's edge. A jogger runs on the sand. I see a tall man playing frisbee with his white dog.

Looking up, I notice the faded bits of yellow and orange stripes in the blue sky. A few clouds still carry that smoky morning look as if they are still sleepy and haven't fluffed up for the day ahead.

Everything looks new and different, yet somehow familiar.

As soon as the truck stops, I jump over the side. Bouncing off the sand, I run towards the waves and reach the water before anyone else.

No one is going to call me a "squid" this morning.

Chapter Eleven
Sea Horse

I stop just short of the water. It's still early. I'm not sure I want to swim. Footsteps patter behind me, and as I turn, Tita grabs my hand and pulls me into the water. Both of us scream at the icy cold water. Goose bumps pop out on my arms and legs.

Frankie gallops into the water behind us, splashing us further.

"Yeah, yeah! Feels great!" He shouts like he wants the whole beach to hear him. "Nice and cold! Love it! Love it!"

Tita starts kicking water at him, and I join in. Frankie gets his revenge by sweeping his big arms through the water, making his own waves to splash us. I'm freezing as I get soaked, but I scoop water right back at him, hoping to get warmer by moving around.

"Is it cold?" Sergio calls. He's standing just above the lines where the water touches the shore.

Suddenly, the three of us start kicking, scooping, and splashing water right at him, and he jumps back. Tita and I laugh like crazy. Frankie makes noises like a cackling chicken.

"Let's go look for shells," Tita suggests. "I want to bring home something special."

"What's the point? You can buy shells in any store around here," Frankie says. He sits down in the shallow water. He yawns, then presses his hands into the sand behind him to support his heavy frame. Legs spread like a V, he raises his face into the sunshine. "I just want to sit here and soak up some rays."

"I'll come with you," I tell Tita. After Sergio's broken promise this morning, I wouldn't dare ask him to stop at a souvenir store before we leave.

Tita and I start walking up the beach. I enjoy glancing over my shoulder to see the waves wash away our footprints almost as soon as we make them. How many millions of footprints does the ocean wash away? I keep getting this feeling of forever at the coast; something I've never felt before.

Tita shrieks and points down. I see the edge of a sand dollar sticking out of the wet

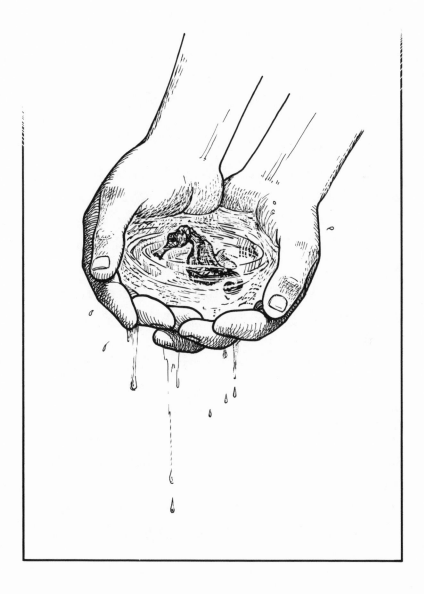

sand. She makes a dive for it. She pulls it out, and we both groan. The shell is only half there. She throws it down, and we keep walking.

The steady winds begin to dry my hair. The sun warms my body. I stop and look out at the ocean again. I take a deep breath, still trying to decide what the beach smells like. I finally decide the sticky, salty, fishy smell means the beach is a place of many surprises. I should have guessed that from the beginning.

I turn so I can catch up to Tita. I glance down, looking for treasures, when a wave washes over a skinny green thing wiggling in the sand. I stop, afraid it might be part of a jellyfish.

I plant my feet on each side of it. My eyes grow big. I have found a very special treasure: a sea horse.

Not sure how to hold it, I finally pick it up by its curly tail. It wiggles like a worm. I gasp, dropping it just as a wave washes in. But I don't want the water to steal my treasure, so I scoop the creature back into my hands.

The sea horse is a mossy green color with glassy eyes and yellow stripes along its tail. It can't be more than two inches long. Its squirming tickles my hand. I rub it gently with my other hand. It feels very different from the fish I caught yesterday. There are no rough scales or a hard shell like the shrimp. It feels more squashy than it looks.

"Tita!" I look up, calling again. "Tita, come look."

She comes running back. "What did you find? Oh! A sea horse! Alicia! Can I touch it?"

Her smaller fingers poke the sea horse. It almost squirms out of my hand. I pull my hand back and cup the other one over it. "I can't hold it forever," I say. "Let's go back and find something to put it in."

As we walk back, Tita's talking about everything she learned in school about sea horses, but I don't pay attention. I'm too busy thinking up ways to keep this treasure alive. Better than a picture of a sunrise, I have a living creature I can keep in my bedroom. I wonder if my parents would buy me an aquarium for my birthday in four months. I wonder if pet stores sell salt water. And food! What would I feed my little sea horse? My mind is swimming with questions.

"Look what Alicia found!" Tita is screaming. "She found a live sea horse."

As we reach the place where Mr. Sandoval and Sergio put up the canvas shade, my sea horse is barely moving.

Carmen picks up Sammy so he can see the sea horse. His stubby little fingers reach out to grab it, but I pull it out of his reach.

Sammy calls me "meanie" because I won't let him hold the sea horse. I have to protect my treasure, and I turn away from his mad face.

"It needs some water," I say. I'm getting worried my sea horse might die.

Meanwhile, Tita fills Sammy's bucket with salt water and brings it back for the sea horse.

I put it in the water. Only the tail moves. I see a wiggle, then a slow uncurling as if it's stretching. But the tail never curves back in. Before long, the sea horse floats to the top like a dead goldfish.

"Is it sleeping?" Sammy asks, bending his dark head over the bucket.

"It's dead," Tita says.

I almost hate her because she says it so easily.

I sit down in the sand and scoop the sea horse back into the palm of my hand. I stroke its tail slowly. My eyes sting. Sand, I guess. Sand and salt water. I can even taste it.

"Dead, huh? Too bad."

Sergio's voice hangs over me like a rain-cloud.

"I can still take it home," I say, wishing he would just leave me alone.

"I don't want a dead sea horse around. It'll stink up my car."

I say nothing. Even if I could seal this horse in plastic so it wouldn't stink up Sergio's car, I'm crazy to think I could keep it in my room. Mom would throw it out immediately or feed it to the cat next door.

Tita sits down beside me. "Why don't you do like the people in the shell shops? In there, the sea horses are hard and dry. And they don't smell. Why don't you lay your sea horse out in the sun? Let it dry out."

I frown at Tita. I'm not one to trust an eight-year-old's great ideas, but I'm feeling desperate. Just to be sure, I get another opinion.

"Sergio, do you think it would work?" I say, then look over my shoulder. I squint into the sun as he walks around me.

"You might as well try it. I won't let you take a wet, dead fish in my car." He laughs like he knows a big secret and I don't.

Then he walks off to where Carmen and Sammy have gone to toss bread pieces to a small flock of sea gulls.

Staring down at the sea horse, I decide to try Tita's plan. It seems like my best chance to take the sea horse home.

Tita finds a frisbee in the back of the truck. "Let's use this."

I lay the sea horse in the center of it.

"Where should we put it?" Tita asks me.

I look around. If I'm depending on the sun to dry out the sea horse, then I know I need to get it as close to the sun as possible.

"Let's put it on the top of the truck," I say.

Tita holds the frisbee as I climb onto the front of the truck. I work fast because the hood of the truck is already hot from the sun. I don't mind my hot feet too much. I know the hotter the sun, the better chance I have for the sun to do its work.

Taking the blue frisbee from Tita, I rest it on top of the truck cab. I say a silent prayer that the sun will dry the fishy smell out of my sea horse.

I jump down and Tita puts her hand on my arm. She's smiling.

"You'll see, Alicia. By the time we're ready to leave after lunch, the sea horse will be dry and crunchy. Come on! Let's go swimming."

I nod, following Tita back to the ocean. She runs off into the waves, but I hear the cries of the sea gulls and turn to watch Carmen, Sergio, and Sammy tossing food to them. Sergio lifts Sammy in his arms so the little boy can throw higher. Both of them laugh when a bird catches what Sammy throws.

Something pulls my attention back to the truck. I explode in a scream. "My sea horse!"

A large sea gull swoops down on the truck and steals my sea horse in its beak. My eyes fill with tears so fast, I barely see the gull fly into the hills. Then, a shadow seems to cover me.

"What's wrong?" Sergio's standing over me.

"That..." I stop to swallow a salty stream, worse than what I tasted when I drank the ocean. "That sea gull ate my sea horse. I lost my sea horse." I turn and look up at my big brother.

Sergio sighs, then shakes his head. "I guess you shouldn't have left it where a sea gull could eat it."

I lower my eyes, trying not to cry. I guess it's impossible for Sergio to care about my feelings.

"Cheer up, Alicia. Maybe you'll find another," Sergio says.

I know the chance of finding another sea horse and getting a different brother are about even. I have a pain in my chest the size of a volleyball.

I turn away from Sergio. With small steps, I splash through the shallow water and walk alone down the beach.

Chapter Twelve
Sergio and Me

I don't walk too far. I don't want to worry Carmen's parents. They've been very nice to me the last two days. Tita and Frankie too. I even like Sammy, and of course, Carmen. I never thought much about big sisters until Carmen started hanging around the house with Sergio. If she and Sergio get married someday, then she'll be my sister-in-law. She'd be part of my family forever. I like that idea a lot.

I stop to face the ocean. I listen to the noise of the waves, like a roar inside a hollow cave. Way in the distance is one of those oil towers. I wish it didn't leak and make tar on the beach. It's so gross. Maybe I should do a school report on oil leaks. I'll bring my bathing suit to show the class what happens on the beach when there's oil in the ocean.

No matter what, I do love the beach. I kick up my foot, watching the water splash up. I let out a loud sigh and tell myself that the hungry sea gull needed his lunch more than I needed a treasure to keep in my room. It only helps a little.

Turning back towards the Sandoval's truck, I push my feet through the water to make the water splash up as I walk. I see Tita and Frankie with the foam board out in the waves. Sammy's digging in the sand with Carmen. Sergio is under the shade, drinking a soda and talking with Mr. and Mrs. Sandoval.

I walk over to where Carmen and Sammy are sitting and squat down beside him.

"Sammy, I'm sorry I didn't let you touch my sea horse," I say.

He looks at me. "Carmen says a sea gull ate it."

I sit down beside him. "Yeah, that's right."

"They eat everything. Even marshmallows!" Sammy says. His voice sounds as if he can't believe it. With his black eyes wide and shiny, he looks so cute. I can't help but smile.

"Alicia, I'm really sorry about your sea horse," Carmen says in her nice, gentle voice.

"It's okay," I say, still smiling because of Sammy. "I was dumb to leave it where a sea gull could eat it."

She pats my arm. "You know, we could stop at a shell shop before we leave and buy you one."

"Are you kidding? Sergio would never stop at a shell shop so I can buy a sea horse."

"Alicia? Of course he would. Just ask him."

The pain in my chest seems to have gone to my head. I can feel my face squeezing together.

"Why should I ask Sergio to stop?" I'm almost yelling at her, but I'm hurting inside and want someone to know it. "He never does what I want to. Only what he wants to. He doesn't care about anyone but himself."

I know that's a lousy thing to say to Carmen. She's found some reason to like Sergio. But I just can't control all this stuff trying to come out.

"Alicia, that's not true," she says. "Your brother cares about you."

"Oh yeah, right. Look at this morning. I really wanted to see the sunrise, but what did he say? No!" I roar out "No" like a lion.

Carmen pops backwards real fast, like I hit her or something. Her eyes get a shadow inside them, and her lips curve downward, like she is the one who ate my sea horse.

113

"What happened this morning was my fault, Alicia. I told Sergio that the sunrise could be very romantic for the two of us. He wanted to please me. I'm sorry. He should have kept his promise to you. Please, don't blame Sergio for my selfishness."

I stare at her with my mouth open. She looks so sad. I didn't think Carmen ever did anything selfish. Then I look at Sammy and remember the way I was about the sea horse. Everyone gets selfish sometimes. Me. Carmen. And yes, Sergio too.

Somehow I feel different. The pain seems to have drained out a tiny hole and gotten soaked up by the sand.

"Why don't you ask Sergio?" Carmen's voice is gentle and sweet again. "Just tell him that you'd like to buy a sea horse. Just talk to him."

"He'll say no. He always says no," I answer.

"He didn't say 'no' when I invited you to the beach, did he?"

"Only because he would have looked mean to you. The two of us aren't like your brothers and sister. We never will be." I say it like it doesn't matter to me, but I know it does.

114

"Maybe you just never pay attention to nice things he does for you," Carmen says. "Think about it."

I didn't want to think about it. If she was right, I'd feel stupid. If she was wrong, I would never have a chance to like my brother at all.

"I want water to make ushy-gushy sand," Sammy says. He gets up with his bucket and goes off towards the water.

About that time, Sergio shows up. He gets down on one knee beside the spot where Carmen sits. His hands squeeze her shoulders. She looks up and smiles at him, and he smiles back. Then he looks at me with that friendly smile still on his mouth. I decide to try things Carmen's way.

"Sergio, since the sea gull ate my sea horse, can we stop at a shell shop and buy me one?"

Sergio's eyes roll. "Shell shop, huh?"

I'm ready to slug him when he rolls his eyes that way, but I make myself ask again. "Can't we stop, Sergio? Please?"

I know the last time I said "please" to my brother, I got disappointed, but I'm anxious to see a shell shop now.

Sergio's frowning, but he nods. "Okay. We'll stop. Just long enough for you to run in and buy a sea horse, okay?"

"Oh, Sergio! Can't you see things from my side? I want to look around a little. I've never been in a shell shop before. Have you?" I stop, surprised at myself. Sergio's eyes open up too.

Then I try to see things from his side. "I know you hate to go shopping, but it's not like going to the mall with the same old stores. A shell shop is different."

"The ferry lines are going to be long," he says.

"Then, we'll go back that other way you wanted to go yesterday," I answer, just to let him know I can be unselfish too.

"Yeah, I guess we could go home a different way." Sergio actually smiles at me. Teeth and everything. "You've never seen Corpus Christi. The bridge over the bay looks cool. And it's also a straight shot back home from there."

"Does that mean we can go to a shell shop?" I ask, just to make sure he didn't change the subject on me.

"Okay, Alicia, we can go."

I smile at Sergio first, then Carmen. "Thanks. Thanks a lot."

"But we won't stay longer than twenty minutes, okay?" he says and lifts up one eyebrow like a question mark.

Good old Sergio. Let's not be too nice, too fast.

I nod. "Sure, okay. Twenty minutes."

"Hey! Alicia!" Frankie calls out.

I turn towards the ocean to see Frankie waving his brown arms at me. He's standing waist deep in the ocean with Tita, who's bobbing through the waves on the float.

Suddenly I feel a sudden gush of cold water on my legs. Sammy has returned and dumped his bucket of water on me while trying to wet the sand. "Ushy-gushy sand! Make sand pies, Carmen."

We all laugh at Sammy as he splats down in the wet sand.

"Make some good pies, Sammy. I'm going swimming," I say, then hop up and run towards the ocean.

I leap through the waves using my arms and legs to make as many splashes as I can. My insides feel like fireworks are shooting off. I promise myself that one day I will come back here and celebrate with salt water sparklers again.

And if he really wants to, Sergio can come too.

Chapter Thirteen
Treasures to Keep

I am really glad Carmen knows the area. With so many souvenir places, I couldn't pick one out for our shopping. Sergio follows her directions and we stop at a place, TREASURES OF THE SEA, a square wooden building with pink flamingos painted on its side.

We walk up a ramp that is supposed to look like a pier and reach the glass doors of the shop.

SUN YOUR BUNS AT PORT ARANSAS I read on the beach towel hanging by the door. Lying under a yellow sun are three pink bunny rabbits wearing sunglasses. One's in a blue bikini, one's in striped shorts, and another's in a yellow bikini. They're each sipping a tall drink, relaxing on beach chairs. Looks like they had a good time too.

Sergio opens the door, and Carmen and I go inside.

Somehow I smell the ocean, but cooler. I guess it's the air-conditioner in the shell shop. I smell bubble gum, suntan lotion, incense. Everything has a scent of some kind, even the rubber sharks piled in a wicker basket by the cashier.

The mobiles tinkle together. They are made of strings of shells hanging from a wooden circle. They move around whenever someone opens the door.

One wall of the store looks wall-papered in T-shirts. They all say something about the beach or ocean or have sea creatures decorating them. On different shirts I see hot orange sunsets sinking into blue green waves. A black shark with its red jaws wide open looks ready to chomp me. There are scuba divers and mermaids, sea horses and blue marlins swimming on yellow, green, and pink shirts. Racks of more shirts follow the wall around to the back of the building.

Above my head, fish nets in bright yellows and pinks hang down from the ceiling. They're filled with beach balls and floating rings. Along the floor are baskets of rubber thongs in all sorts of sizes. There are more rubber toys: eels, snakes, squid, and fish. Someone Sammy's age would love it here.

Carmen wanders off to look at a display of jewelry, earrings and necklaces made of shells or coral. Sergio stops to look at carvings of birds and fish made of driftwood. I go past the racks of postcards to discover the treasures on tables.

I have never seen so many shells in all my life. Sea shells are everywhere. All colors, shapes, and sizes. Each shell has its own special look. How can anybody choose one over another?

I pick up a sand dollar and run my fingers over the cross design. It's so delicate and fragile. I put it down carefully.

I smile when I see a hundred dry little sea horses piled in a flat basket on the table. One feels prickly on my fingertips.

Now I understand what Tita meant about a dried sea horse. I decide the one I lost was too special to replace. I move on to the next table.

I go past shelves of little animals and people made of shells. I examine the little fan shells for bodies, round hermit crab shells for heads, pipe cleaner hands and two plastic eyes glued on the tiny faces.

I laugh when I look at the back wall and see the display of carved coconut heads. One has big red lips puckered up for a giant kiss. The one beside it has a pirate's scarf and a black patch over one eye. Another has blue hair sticking out of its head and big round eyes like it saw something that scared it silly. Each face has its own personality. I admire the lady who carved these heads. She must have had a lot of fun.

I turn the corner and find a shelf of books, and that's where Sergio and Carmen find me later.

"Are you ready to go?" Carmen asks me.

"Huh?" I look up from the book I'm reading and blink at her.

"What are you looking at?" Sergio asks.

"A book with stories about things people believe about the ocean. Sea monsters, haunted ships. Mysteries no one has solved." I close the book and smile. "I think I'm going to take it."

"Think you can solve all the mysteries, right?" Sergio says.

I almost stick my tongue out at him, but instead I tell him,

"Maybe I will solve a mystery. You never know." I move away, heading towards the cashier.

"Aren't you going to buy a shell or sea horse or something?" Carmen asks as we walk down the aisle past all the sea treasures.

"There are too many to choose from. Sammy gave me two of his shells. I'll just keep those," I tell her.

The shells I packed in my suitcase were egg-colored scallops, and nothing like the shiny, smooth shells around me, but I will treasure them more. Sammy found them on the beach before we left today. They will remind me of new things I discovered during this first trip to the beach.

As I get money out of my pocket, I want to laugh at myself.

I come to a shell shop, but don't buy any shells. Seems like from the very beginning, things worked out like this. I had all these silly ideas about what the beach is. Then, things weren't like I thought, but it was still terrific. Even having Sergio around didn't turn out too bad.

No, I wouldn't have traded a moment of this trip for all the beautiful shells in the world. I'll just take what I've got and go back home. And share my story with everyone.

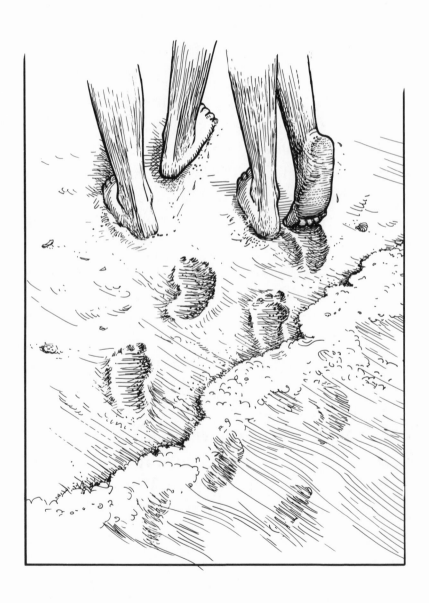

About the Author

Diane Gonzales Bertrand wrote her first novel into a spiral notebook when she was in fifth grade. During high school and college, she kept adding chapters until the novel filled over fifty notebooks. When she became a school teacher, she wrote plays for her students and helped them write and perform their own poems and plays.

In 1992, Ms. Bertrand earned her Masters Degree in English, and began working at St. Mary's University, where she teaches creative writing and English composition. She has published many poems and essays, and has written three novels that were published by Avalon Books. Her fourth novel, *Sweet Fifteen*, was published by Piñata Books in 1995.

Ms. Bertrand continues to reside in her home town, San Antonio, Texas. In addition to teaching and writing, she enjoys reading books with her two children and helping her husband with their family-owned business.